ROCKFORD PUBLIC LIBRARY

W9-BJS-643

3 1112 018699021

E PAR
Parish, Herman
Amelia Bedelia tries her
luck

082813

WITHDRAWN

ROCKFORD PUBLIC LIBRARY
Rockford, Illinois
www.rockfordpubliclibrary.org
815-965-9511

Dear Parent:
Your child's love of reading starts here!

Every child learns to read in a different way and at his or her own speed. Some go back and forth between reading levels and read favorite books again and again. Others read through each level in order. You can help your young reader improve and become more confident by encouraging his or her own interests and abilities. From books your child reads with you to the first books he or she reads alone, there are I Can Read Books for every stage of reading:

SHARED READING
Basic language, word repetition, and whimsical illustrations, ideal for sharing with your emergent reader

BEGINNING READING
Short sentences, familiar words, and simple concepts for children eager to read on their own

READING WITH HELP
Engaging stories, longer sentences, and language play for developing readers

READING ALONE
Complex plots, challenging vocabulary, and high-interest topics for the independent reader

ADVANCED READING
Short paragraphs, chapters, and exciting themes for the perfect bridge to chapter books

I Can Read Books have introduced children to the joy of reading since 1957. Featuring award-winning authors and illustrators and a fabulous cast of beloved characters, I Can Read Books set the standard for beginning readers.

A lifetime of discovery begins with the magical words "I Can Read!"

Visit www.icanread.com for information on enriching your child's reading experience.

For Angelina—"Just my lucky!"
—H. P.

To Cortney, Tyson, Mayson, and Jonah,
I'm lucky to have you for neighbors!
—L. A.

Gouache and black pencil were used to prepare the full-color art.

I Can Read Book® is a trademark of HarperCollins Publishers.

Amelia Bedelia is a registered trademark of Peppermint Partners, LLC.

Amelia Bedelia Tries Her Luck. Text copyright © 2013 by Herman S. Parish III. Illustrations copyright © 2013 by Lynne Avril. All rights reserved. No part of this book may be used or reproduced in any manner whatsoever without written permission except in the case of brief quotations embodied in critical articles and reviews. Printed in the United States of America. For information address HarperCollins Children's Books, a division of HarperCollins Publishers, 10 East 53rd Street, New York, NY 10022.
www.icanread.com

Library of Congress Cataloging-in-Publication Data is available.

13 14 15 16 17 LP/WOR 10 9 8 7 6 5 4 3 2 1 First Edition
Greenwillow Books

Amelia Bedelia
·Tries Her Luck·

by Herman Parish ✿ pictures by Lynne Avril

Greenwillow Books, *An Imprint of* HarperCollins*Publishers*

ROCKFORD PUBLIC LIBRARY

Amelia Bedelia was getting ready

to go to school when . . .

CRASH!

"I'm sorry!" said Amelia Bedelia.

"Accidents happen, sweetie,"

said her mother.

"The important thing

is that you are not hurt."

At school, Amelia Bedelia told her friends
about the accident.

"You're in trouble," said Clay.
"Breaking a mirror means
seven years of bad luck."

7 7 7

"Seven years!"
said Amelia Bedelia.
"That's almost my whole life!"

"Even worse," said Rose.

"Today is Friday the thirteenth.

Bad luck gets doubled today."

"That's fourteen years!"

said Amelia Bedelia.

"I'll have bad luck forever!"

9

"Amelia Bedelia," said Joy,

"you can change your luck."

"That's right," said Heather.

"My dad always says,

See a penny, pick it up,

all the day you'll have good luck."

Amelia Bedelia picked up Penny.

"Put me down!" said Penny.

"Heather means a penny coin,

not a Penny person."

At recess, the whole class
tried to help Amelia Bedelia
change her luck.

They searched
for a four-leaf clover.

They looked for
a lucky horseshoe.

They tried to find a rabbit's foot.

The playground didn't have any of
those things.

"I'm sorry, Amelia Bedelia," said Clay.
"We struck out. You are out of luck."

Amelia Bedelia made a plan.

If she could not find luck,

she would make her own luck.

15

Amelia Bedelia's teacher, Miss Edwards,

saw her drawings.

She also saw that Amelia Bedelia was upset.

"Are you all right?" asked Miss Edwards.

"No, I am all wrong,"
said Amelia Bedelia.
She told Miss Edwards
about breaking the mirror
and her double bad luck.

"Amelia Bedelia," said Miss Edwards,
"today is my lucky day.
Friday the thirteenth
is the perfect day
to talk about luck."

The class listed lucky and unlucky things.

They talked about bad luck and good luck.

There were all kinds of questions.

itions

Good Luck
4 Leaf Clover
Horseshoe
Blowing out candles on
birthday Cake

Miss Edwards told the class a story.

"When I was your age," she said,

"One saying really scared me.

It was, *Step on a crack,*

break your mother's back."

"That's terrible," said Amelia Bedelia.

"But it isn't true," said Miss Edwards.

"Just like breaking a mirror isn't bad luck."

"Breaking a mirror is bad luck," said Clay.

"It's bad luck for the mirror!"

Everyone laughed.

Amelia Bedelia laughed hardest of all.

She felt a lot better.

As Amelia Bedelia was walking home,
she saw a crack in the sidewalk.
"Bad luck? Ha!" she said.

She stepped on the crack.

She stepped on every crack she saw.

When she spied the biggest one of all,

Amelia Bedelia stomped on it.

Then Amelia Bedelia turned onto her street, and she stopped in her tracks.

There was an ambulance

in front of her house.

Amelia Bedelia raced home.

Breaking the mirror was an accident,

but she had stepped on those cracks

on purpose.

"Mom!" yelled Amelia Bedelia.

"I didn't mean to break your back!"

The ambulance was pulling away.

"Mom!" cried Amelia Bedelia. "Mom!"

"Amelia Bedelia!" said her mother.

"I'm with Mrs. Adams, sweetie."

Amelia Bedelia whirled around.

Her mom was with their neighbor.

Her back was fine!

Amelia Bedelia ran to her mom.

She gave her the biggest,

longest, strongest hug ever.

"Ouch, honey!"

said Amelia Bedelia's mother.

"Do you want to break my back?"

"No, never!" said Amelia Bedelia.

"You just missed the excitement,"
said Mrs. Adams.
"I got a ride home in an ambulance
after my checkup."

"Are you okay?" asked Amelia Bedelia.
"I am fine," said Mrs. Adams.
"Knock on wood."

Then Mrs. Adams knocked three times
on her porch railing.

Tomorrow, Amelia Bedelia would add
"knock on wood" to the list
her class had made.
Today, worrying about luck
had worn her out.

Amelia Bedelia thought about
her family and her great friends.
She thought that the mirror
Mrs. Adams gave her was cool.

Amelia Bedelia felt like she was
the luckiest person in the world.